My Naughty Little Puppy

Rascal's Festive Fun

Wag! Wag!

For everyone who's adopted
a second-chance pet from
a rescue centre ~ H.W.
For Sue and Geoff ~ K.P.

WOOF
magazine

STRIPES PUBLISHING
An imprint of Magi Publications
1 The Coda Centre,
189 Munster Road,
London SW6 6AW

A paperback original
First published in Great Britain
in 2011

Text copyright © Holly Webb, 2011
Illustrations copyright
© Kate Pankhurst, 2011

ISBN: 978-1-84715-198-8

The right of Holly Webb and Kate
Pankhurst to be identified as the
author and illustrator of this work
respectively has been asserted by
them in accordance with the
Copyright, Designs and Patents
Act, 1988.

A CIP catalogue record for this
book is available from the British
Library.

Printed and bound in the UK.

10 9 8 7 6 5 4 3 2 1

My Naughty Little Puppy

HOLLY WEBB

Illustrated by
Kate Pankhurst

stripes

Chapter One

Christmas Wishes

"Your turn, Ellie!" Dad handed over the wooden spoon, and Ellie knelt on her chair to reach the huge mixing bowl. She breathed in the delicious smell of spices and orange peel. It felt like it was almost Christmas already – there were only a couple of weeks to go!

"Don't forget to make a wish," her big sister Lila reminded her.

Ellie frowned as she stirred the spoon

My Naughty Little Puppy

slowly round and round. What should she wish for? Last year she had wished for a puppy, of course – she had wished for a puppy every time she blew out her birthday candles, or saw a shooting star, and every Christmas when she stirred the pudding mixture. But now she had Rascal. What else could Ellie possibly want?

My Naughty Little Puppy

She looked round the kitchen thoughtfully, searching for something to help her out.

"Hurry up, Ellie, it must be my turn now," Max moaned.

"Just a minute," Ellie murmured. "Oh!" she whispered to herself, as she spotted the leaflet that had come through the door that morning. She'd pinned it up on the kitchen noticeboard because it had a gorgeous picture of a Jack Russell on it, a wire-haired one, not a smooth-coated one like Rascal.

The leaflet was from Paws for Thought, the animal shelter a few streets away from Ellie's school. They took in abandoned or unwanted dogs and cats – and even a python once, the leaflet said. Someone had just left the enormous snake in a cardboard

box on the doorstep. The leaflet said the
Jack Russell on the front was called Brady,
and he was about five years old. They didn't
know exactly, because Brady had been
found wandering along the riverbank, where
he'd been abandoned.

Ellie had looked at his photo for a long
time, and then all the other dogs with their
photos inside. They all looked so sweet
and so hopeful, as though the very next
person who walked in might take them
home and love them.

She'd put the leaflet up so she didn't
forget. Partly she wanted to remember
how lucky they were to have Rascal and
to be able to look after him properly, but
also she wanted to do something to help

the shelter. She just hadn't worked out what yet. The back of the leaflet explained that they didn't just need new homes for the animals, they needed donations too, to pay for the food and the vet's bills.

Ellie closed her eyes tightly, and wished as hard as she could. *Please let Brady find a home soon. And Scamper, and Lottie, and Patrick, and all the others...*

She then handed the spoon to Max. "About time too," Max said. "This smells so good, Mum. Can't we just have Christmas pudding for tea today?"

"No, you have to keep it for a while, it tastes better that way," Mum explained. "That's why we make it a few weeks before Christmas. Have you made your wish, Max?

My Naughty Little Puppy

Now everyone's had a turn stirring, we can put the charms in. I've got a new one this year." She opened up a tin, and unwrapped the silvery charms from their cushion of tissue paper. There was a ring for marriage, a horseshoe for good luck, a sixpence for riches, and a wishbone for a wish. "And here's the new one," she added, dropping a tiny silver dog into the tin. "I saw it when I was out shopping, and I couldn't resist."

My Naughty Little Puppy

"Oh, it's so cute!" Ellie smiled. "It looks just like Rascal!"

"Doesn't it?" Mum agreed. "Now we just need to tie some ribbon on to them, so no one accidentally eats one."

"Hang on, Mum," Lila said thoughtfully. "What does the dog charm mean? All the others have got meanings. Like the lucky horseshoe."

Mum nodded slowly. "Yes, I hadn't thought about that."

"Maybe whoever gets it has to walk Rascal for a week!" Max suggested.

"Ellie always wants to walk him anyway!" Dad laughed.

"How about they have to clean up whatever mess Rascal makes for a week instead?" Mum said grimly. "Actually, where *is* Rascal?"

"Isn't he asleep on his cushion?" Ellie said, turning round to look.

But Rascal's big red dog cushion was empty. Only a few white hairs were scattered across it. No cute Jack Russell puppy.

Everyone looked around the kitchen anxiously. Rascal loved people, and he especially loved Ellie. So when he disappeared and even Ellie didn't know where he was, it almost always meant he was doing something naughty.

"What's that noise?" Lila asked suddenly.

It was a squelchy sort of noise. Gungy. Like someone chewing something that was very, very sticky.

My Naughty Little Puppy

Ellie sighed and bent down to peer under the table.

"Hi, Rascal," she said, not sounding very surprised. "Um, Mum? Did we want any cherries in the Christmas pudding?"

Everyone else crouched down to look too, and Rascal stared back at them and wagged his tail. He took a guilty step back from the empty tub of glacé cherries and sat down, trying to look innocent.

He wasn't very convincing.

Chapter Two

Ellie's Brilliant Idea

"Well done, everyone! All the puppies worked really hard today." Jo beamed around the whole class at the end of dog training the next day. Ellie bent down to pat Rascal's head, feeling very proud. Quite often she came out of dog training knowing that they'd definitely learned lots, but wishing Rascal hadn't weed on the floor, or eaten someone's sandwiches, or slipped his lead and disappeared into the mop cupboard...

My Naughty Little Puppy

But today he'd been perfect. It was just as well. Mum still hadn't forgiven him for eating all the glacé cherries. She said they were a vital part of the recipe and that the Christmas pudding would taste completely different now. Ellie wasn't sure she remembered cherries being in it before, but she'd decided it would be best not to say so.

"Just before you go..." Ellie looked up as Jo carried on talking. "I've got this poster I'm putting up. Some of you might know that I volunteer at Paws for Thought, the animal shelter? I help out, take the dogs for walks, that sort of thing. They're having a Christmas Fair here next Sunday."

Ellie nodded. "We had a leaflet through the door at the weekend."

"Yes, they really need to boost their funds. And, of course, they're worried they'll get lots more puppies soon after Christmas." Jo sighed at the thought of dogs becoming unwanted presents. "Anyway, please come, and tell all your friends!"

Ellie led Rascal back over to Dad, who was waiting at the side of the hall. "Did you see how good Rascal was?" she asked happily.

"He was a little star today," Dad agreed. "Especially at the sit and stay – I couldn't believe he sat there for so long, even with Jo trying to distract him."

My Naughty Little Puppy

"Are you going to go to this Christmas
Fair, Ellie?" Jack came over with his
enormous Great Dane, Hugo. Hugo was
well-named – he seemed to get huger
every time Ellie saw him. "I think it sounds
fun. I looked at the poster and it said lots of
the stalls will have cool things for dogs."

My Naughty Little Puppy

"We can, can't we, Dad?" Ellie asked.
"I'd really like to go. And we could bring
Mum and Lila and Max too. Oh! And
maybe I could get Grandad a Christmas
present, if there are dog pictures and things
like that. He loves dogs." Ellie's grandad
was very fond of Rascal, and he'd given Ellie
lots of good advice about him. It had been
Grandad who'd suggested Rascal needed
to go to dog training in the first place.

Ellie and Dad walked home quickly.
It was too cold to linger, and even Rascal
didn't seem to want to stop and sniff
exciting smells as often as usual.

"I wonder if it'll snow soon!" Ellie said
excitedly. It was so cold, they might even
have a white Christmas.

My Naughty Little Puppy

Dad looked up at the dark, cloudy sky. "You never know," he agreed. "It did snow last year. Though most of it came after Christmas, didn't it?"

Ellie danced on ahead with Rascal, thinking about snow, and the Christmas holidays. Even before the holidays began, there was all the fun stuff to do at school. They were having the final rehearsals for the Christmas play, and they'd been learning lots of Christmas songs.

"'Dashing through the snow, in a one-horse open sleigh...'" Ellie sang happily, and Rascal joined in with an excited little yip. "Are you singing too, Rascal?" she said, patting him.

"That sounded really good, Ellie!"

My Naughty Little Puppy

Dad laughed, as they reached their gate. "Very festive! That reminds me, we'd better go and get our Christmas tree at the weekend."

"Ooooh, yes," Ellie agreed, as they walked up the path. Then she stopped suddenly, halfway to the front door. "Dad, I've just had a brilliant idea! Me and Jack and some of the others from dog training could sing carols at the Christmas Fair! That would get everyone in a Christmassy mood, wouldn't it?"

Dad nodded. "It does sound like a good idea. Why don't you suggest it to Jo at the Thursday class?" He looked at her hopefully. "Ellie, shall we go into the house now? My toes are about to freeze off!"

Chapter Three

Crafty Christmas

"That sounds like a really cool idea," Christy said, as she carefully sprinkled red glitter on to the photo frame she was making. Miss Wright was letting them do lots of Christmas crafts now that it was the last week of term.

"I hope Jo says yes. It would get everyone feeling really Christmassy, and then they'd want to go and buy loads of presents and things!" Ellie smiled. "Did you get a leaflet about the shelter at the weekend?

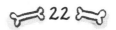

My Naughty Little Puppy

They really need to raise some money."

Christy nodded. "It was so sad!
All those dogs with no proper homes.
I showed it to Mum and Dad, but they said
one dog was enough, especially when he's
as big as Bouncer." Bouncer was Christy's
golden Labrador. He was gorgeous and
very well-behaved, but there was no
denying that he took up a lot of room.

"We got one too," Lucy put in. "They
must have delivered them all over town.
Some of the dogs looked really sweet."

Ellie smiled at her. Lucy wasn't a huge
dog fan – she'd been quite scared of them
until she'd come to Ellie's birthday
sleepover, and Rascal had "adopted" her.
It was as though he'd known Lucy was

scared, and he'd done everything he could to prove how nice dogs can be.

"Are you excited about this afternoon?" Ellie asked her, and Lucy nodded, wrinkling her nose.

"Excited but scared at the same time. I woke up in the middle of the night and I was certain it was all going to go wrong! But I felt better about my solo this morning when I saw my costume again – it's so pretty."

Lucy had joined their school in the summer term, and had quickly made friends with Ellie and Christy. She was a brilliant dancer, and a few weeks ago she'd been showing them one of her ballet exam pieces in the playground when Miss Wright, their new teacher for Year Four, had spotted her.

My Naughty Little Puppy

When the rehearsals for the Christmas play started, Lucy found out that she'd been cast as a snowflake, with a solo dance to do. It was the dress rehearsal that afternoon, and the show was tomorrow evening.

Ellie was actually quite glad she was only an elf in the play. She had one line to say, "The dark forest is that way!" and lots of songs and a bit of dancing. That was quite enough. She loved being in plays, but she didn't want to be centre-stage like Lucy, or Christy, who was an elf too, but with loads of words to say.

"Ellie, that's beautiful!" Miss Wright was leaning over their table. "Really clever, the way you've built up the layers so the holly leaves look solid."

"Thank you!" Ellie stuck another bead on to the picture frame. They were making them as presents for their parents. Miss Wright had taken photos of them in their play costumes to put inside. As Ellie was meant to be a holly elf, she'd cut out holly leaves to go all round the frame. She was using red beads as berries, and she was really pleased with it.

My Naughty Little Puppy

"There's the bell for lunch, everyone."
Miss Wright looked round at the glittery
classroom, rather worriedly. "Oh well. Just
put your frames over on this table to.dry.
And after lunch, come straight back here
to put your costumes on!"

Luckily, they were so busy with the play all
afternoon that Miss Wright had decided it
would be mean to give them homework
too. Ellie and Christy walked home
together, with Ellie's mum and Rascal.
When they got to the hill just before their
road, Rascal raced ahead. He dragged
Ellie, who was holding his lead, behind
him, and Christy had to run alongside them.

My Naughty Little Puppy

"I am sooo tired," Ellie panted, as they reached the top of the hill. "All I want to do is go and flop on the sofa! I hope pulling me up the hill's tired you out too, Rascal. I'm not sure I can face another walk tonight."

Rascal looked up hopefully at the word "walk", and Ellie sighed.

"I need to practise my words again for tomorrow," Christy said. "See you in the morning, Ellie!"

When she got in, Ellie took her photo frame out of her bag and sneaked upstairs to hide it in her bedroom. She slipped it into the big box under her bed, where she was keeping all the presents she'd got for everyone, and looked down at it happily. She was sure Mum and Dad would like it.

Rascal put his paws
up on the edge of the
box, and sniffed
at the frame
interestedly.
It smelled of
glue, and the red
beads looked juicy.

"No, it's not for eating,
Rascal!" Ellie quickly put the lid back on
and pushed the box back under the bed.
"You like it too, mmm?" She looked down
at him thoughtfully. "Maybe I could do
another one for Grandad and put a
photo of you inside! That would be a
lovely present!"

She looked around for the camera her

mum and dad had given her for her birthday, and then shook her head. "I need to make you look really Christmassy first..." she told Rascal.

Rascal stared back at her, bright-eyed and hopeful. He was still sure those beads would have been delicious.

Chapter Four

Rascal's Photoshoot

"Mum, have you got any red material I can borrow?" Ellie hovered next to her mum's mini-office under the stairs.

"I might have, why?" Mum glanced round from her computer. She'd told Ellie she needed to get a bit of work finished off before she made the dinner.

Ellie rubbed one foot up and down her leg, and smiled. "It's sort of a secret," she admitted.

"Oh, really...? Well, I suppose you can go and have a look through that bag of scraps in the back of my wardrobe – actually, no, hang on, I'll get it for you." Mum jumped up hurriedly, and Ellie grinned. There were definitely things in Mum's wardrobe that she didn't want anyone to see!

"Will this do?" Mum asked her a few minutes later, waving a piece of bright red felt round the door.

"Oooh, yes!" Ellie stroked it delightedly. "That's perfect. Can I really have it?"

"It was left over from some costume Max had to have for school. Yes, you have it, Ellie. Just don't get red fluff all over your bedroom!"

"OK! Thanks, Mum." Ellie went back to

My Naughty Little Puppy

her room, where Rascal was now curled up snoozing on her bed. Ellie had a close look at him, especially his ears. She knew exactly what she wanted to end up with, but she wasn't quite sure how to make it.

She fetched the scissors from the little sewing box that Gran and Grandpa had given her last Christmas, and spread the red fabric out on the floor. Luckily, it had a sort of plasticky backing, so she wouldn't need to hem it or do anything too complicated. She took a deep breath and started carefully cutting.

Half an hour later, she had something that really looked like a dog-sized Santa hat. With ear-holes. Ellie looked at it proudly. She'd found some cotton wool

in her sewing box that Mum had given her
to use as snow on the Christmas cards
she'd made last year. There was just
enough to go around the brim of the hat,
and make a little pompom for the top.

Rascal had woken up, and was now
sitting next to her on the floor, occasionally
sniffing at the white fluffy stuff. It made him
sneeze.

"Want to try it on, Rascal?" Ellie
suggested, holding it out.

Rascal eyed the hat doubtfully. He wasn't
absolutely sure what it was, although he liked
the way it dangled about. Was it a new toy?

"Sit still a minute," Ellie told him, putting
the hat on his head and gently arranging
his ears in the holes. "Ohhh, Rascal, you

look so funny! Let me take a photo of you!"
She turned to grab the camera.

Rascal shook his head uncertainly. It felt
very odd. The hat slipped down over one
eye, and the bobble bounced in front of his
nose. He seized it in his teeth and nibbled at
it, looking very confused.

Ellie giggled as she took shot after shot of
Rascal in his hat. She wasn't sure she'd ever
get him to wear it again, once he worked out
how to get it off, so she needed to be quick.

My Naughty Little Puppy

But by the time he'd tugged the hat off completely, she had lots of cute pictures. Admittedly, Rascal didn't actually have the hat on straight in a single one, but Ellie didn't think it mattered. He looked more like himself with a wonky hat and a chewed bobble, somehow...

"I'm sure we need more rehearsals," Lucy said worriedly. "We all went the wrong way in the final dance yesterday. It's going to be a disaster!"

Ellie put an arm round her friend. "No, it isn't! It was only a little mistake."

She glanced around. It was lunchtime, but the playground was strangely quiet.

My Naughty Little Puppy

Everyone was huddled about, looking over their words, or practising dance steps. They were doing the play for the infants that afternoon, and then all their parents were coming that evening.

"Everyone's nervous," Christy agreed. "I keep forgetting my lines. But Miss Wright said the rehearsal was great, Lucy."

Ellie burrowed in her coat pocket. "Here, look. I brought these to show you two." She had printed out the photos of Rascal she'd taken the night before. They were so cute she couldn't resist showing her friends!

My Naughty Little Puppy

"He's so funny!" Lucy giggled, looking at the one where Rascal had managed to get the hat over both eyes. "Thanks, Ellie, that's really cheered me up!"

Ellie's mum and dad had even persuaded Max and Lila to come and see the play. When the curtains drew open that night, Ellie could see them all sitting in the second row, with Grandad. Mum was waving, but Ellie only gave her a quick smile back. Miss Wright had made them promise not to get distracted by anyone in the audience.

The play seemed to race along, and it was no time at all before the audience were applauding at the end. Ellie had seen

My Naughty Little Puppy

Mum and Dad beaming as she said her line, and even Max was clapping. When the dancers came on to bow, with Lucy in the middle, people cheered. Lucy looked delighted, and Ellie hugged her as they ran off stage.

"I told you it would all be OK," cried Ellie. "You were a star!"

Chapter Five

Canine Chorus

"Last night was so much fun!" Ellie smiled, and then she gave a huge yawn.

Christy smiled at her and then she yawned too, and so did Lucy. "Oh, it's catching!"

Looking round the classroom, Ellie could tell that everyone was tired after the play last night. They'd slogged through Literacy, and then Miss Wright had announced they were making Christmas decorations, as there were only a couple more days until the end of term. Ellie had enjoyed making Rascal's hat so much that she'd chosen to make the more complicated decoration, a felt stocking decorated with sewn-on sequins. But she was so sleepy she kept dropping the sequins and having to scrabble around on the floor for them.

"What did your teacher think about the carols idea?" Lucy asked. "Have you had another dog-training class yet?"

"No, they're Mondays and Thursdays at the moment," Ellie explained. "It's our last class before Christmas tonight. Oh, I hope she says yes!"

"It's definitely a good idea," Christy said thoughtfully. "But it would be even

My Naughty Little Puppy

better if there was a way to make it more about dogs. Are there any Christmas carols with dogs in them?"

Ellie frowned. "I don't think so," she said at last. "'Rudolf the Red-nosed Reindeer' is the only one I can think of with any animals. Oh, and 'Little Donkey'."

"I know!" Christy sat bolt upright, looking more awake than she had all morning. "Why don't you all take your dogs with you? They can stand next to you while you're singing. And you can put Santa hats on them, like the one you made for Rascal!"

"That's brilliant, Christy!" Ellie said. "Seeing dogs with nice homes would make everybody think about how sad it is for the dogs at the shelter. I'm not sure about the

My Naughty Little Puppy

hats though. We can try, but you saw the photos – Rascal wouldn't keep his on properly at all. And ever since then he's decided it's his new favourite toy. He carries it around everywhere in his mouth!"

"Bouncer would wear a hat, I'm sure he would," Christy said. "I got him a pair of antlers to wear on Christmas Day last year, and he did keep them on for a bit!"

My Naughty Little Puppy

Ellie bounced in her chair excitedly. "I know! If we do it, why don't you bring him too? And his antlers?" Ellie suggested. "I bet Jo wouldn't mind – the more the merrier. And you've been learning all the carols at school..."

"Do you think I could come too, Ellie?" Lucy asked shyly. "I know I haven't got a dog, but I'd really like to help the Christmas Fair go well, so they raise lots of money for the shelter. I could even help you work out dance moves to go with some of the carols, if you like – easy ones, that you could still do if you were holding a lead."

"That would be great!" Ellie beamed at them both. "Would you really both come and help? It'll be even more fun then.

My Naughty Little Puppy

You've met Jack, Christy, he's really nice. I'll
bet he'll come and sing. Hugo would look
fab in a hat!" She giggled. "A big one!"

Jo had planned a Christmassy obstacle
course for the last dog-training session of the
term. The dogs and owners had to walk
round a trail of little paper Christmas trees,
and do various challenges on the way.
It was very funny, especially when Hugo
tried to run through the tube, and forgot
how big he was. Jack had to rescue him,
as he was wandering around with the tube
on his head.

The trickiest bit was the stopping and
staying, because there were Santa-shaped

My Naughty Little Puppy

dog biscuits, which the dogs were supposed to ignore. But all the dogs got one of the biscuits at the end, even Rascal, who'd already eaten two on the way round.

At the end of the session, Jo gathered them all together to give out a note about next term, and remind them about the Christmas Fair on Sunday afternoon.

Ellie waved a hand excitedly. "Jo, I've had an idea for the fair! Could we all bring our dogs, and stand in the entrance hall and sing carols as people are coming in? To get everyone in a Christmas mood? We could even give the dogs Christmassy things to wear, if they wanted. My friend Christy said she'd bring her dog Bouncer too, if that's all right, and he's got some reindeer antlers." She finished on a sort of gasp, as she'd rattled it all off without taking a breath.

Jo was smiling, and the other members of the class were nodding interestedly.

My Naughty Little Puppy

"That's a brilliant idea, Ellie!" said Jo. "I'll ask Carol from the shelter, but I'm sure she'd be really pleased to have you all helping."

Jack looked really excited. Ellie had told him about her idea at the beginning of the class. "Jo, I bet my mum would make Hugo a red dog coat to wear!"

"Oh good." Ellie looked round at the rest of the dog owners, feeling a bit shy. "Do you think we could rehearse some carols quickly tomorrow evening, Jo? Is the hall free?"

"I've got my advanced classes here on Friday nights, but I don't mind if you're in the entrance, practising."

"That's a lovely idea, Ellie!" one of the other owners came over to say. Ellie had seen Tara working in the baker's close to school; she had a really gorgeous Dalmatian called Libby. "I'm going to see if I can make Libby a Christmassy-looking scarf – I don't think she'd wear antlers! I guess we don't need to bring the dogs tomorrow night to rehearse, do we?"

Ellie shook her head. It felt funny organizing all these adults – but at least everyone seemed to love her idea! Amelia was the only one looking grumpy, and Ellie guessed that she wished she was the one getting all the attention.

As Ellie gathered her things to go home, Jack came over, looking thoughtful.

"Are you OK?" Ellie asked.

Jack nodded. "Hugo came from a shelter, you know. Not Paws for Thought,

My Naughty Little Puppy

a different one. I couldn't leave him there. Mum said he was too big, but I begged her." He glanced up at Ellie. "I actually cried in the middle of the shelter. In front of everyone. That's what made her change her mind." He frowned for a second, as though he shouldn't really have admitted that.

Ellie nodded. "Even seeing the dogs in the leaflet made me feel sad. But Mum says no more dogs. No way. One's

enough. But since I can't give any of the dogs a home, I really wanted to do something to help the shelter."

My Naughty Little Puppy

When they got home, Dad helped Ellie find words for the carols on the internet. Then she called Lucy and Christy to tell them the good news, and check they could make the rehearsal.

"I'll work out some moves now!" Lucy told her excitedly. "And you, me and Christy can practise tomorrow at break – it'll be a cool thing to do on the last day of school!"

Ellie could hear Christy dancing around when she told her. "Yay! I can't wait! I went and found Bouncer's antlers just in case!"

Chapter Six

Tree Time

The next morning Lucy dashed up to Ellie and Christy in the playground, waving several sheets of paper with all her ideas on. Soon half the girls in their class were doing the moves.

"When's the Christmas Fair, Ellie?" Lydia asked. "I definitely want to come."

The excitement lasted all day – until Ellie, Lucy and Christy arrived at the hall that evening, and saw Amelia going in.

My Naughty Little Puppy

"Ugh, I'd forgotten she went to your dog training..." Christy moaned. "It's been great not having her at school any more. At least she wasn't in our class, but she was always making nasty comments about people."

Ellie nodded. "I was hoping she wouldn't turn up. Oh well."

"There you are!" Amelia snapped, as soon as Ellie and the others walked in. "I'm doing a solo."

Ellie shrugged. "OK." Christy glared at her, but Ellie muttered, "Let's just keep her happy." She smiled shyly as Tara came in, and a couple of the others.

Jack dashed in last of all. "Sorry, Hugo ate my dinner! Mum had to make me some more. Have you started?"

My Naughty Little Puppy

Ellie grinned, handing him a carol sheet. "No. Here, have some words. And Lucy's come up with some brilliant moves. Things we can do even if we're holding a lead!"

Jack looked worried. "How am I going to hold Hugo and the words, *and* dance?"

"Especially as you can't even walk without tripping up half the time," Amelia muttered.

My Naughty Little Puppy

Christy glared at her, and Lucy smiled at Jack. "It's OK. You know 'Jingle Bells', don't you? You won't need to hold the words for that one."

An hour later, everyone had got the hang of the words, and most of the moves, although Jack still wasn't sure about dancing. "At least no one will be able to see me behind Hugo, anyway," he pointed out.

"I wish we hadn't had to give Amelia a solo," Christy grumbled, as they watched her stalk out.

"I know," Ellie sighed. "She does sing well, though."

"She's good," Lucy admitted, as if she didn't really want to. "Oh well. It's only one verse."

My Naughty Little Puppy

Christy sniffed. "You wait. She'll probably have taken over the whole thing by Sunday."

Christy's mum was dropping them home. Ellie jumped out of the car and dashed into the house, expecting Rascal to be jumping up and down at the door. He wasn't used to her being out in the evening. But there wasn't even an excited bark. Ellie went upstairs, feeling slightly worried.

As she pushed open her bedroom door, Rascal slunk out from under her bed.

"Oh no!" Ellie crouched down. The lid of the big box where she'd been keeping the presents was on the floor. "I should have known you could get that lid off," she muttered. "Oh, Rascal! Max's fudge!"

My Naughty Little Puppy

Rascal wagged his tail happily. It was very good fudge.

Ellie sighed. "I'd be cross with you if I wasn't so happy you're mine, and not stuck in a shelter somewhere," she whispered, hugging him tight.

The next day, Dad dragged Ellie out of bed early. He'd already fed Rascal, who'd followed him upstairs and was dancing around Ellie's bedroom.

"But it's the first day of the holidays!" Ellie wailed.

My Naughty Little Puppy

"Remember," said Dad. "Christmas tree shopping! We want to get one early, then we'll have lots of time for decorating."

Ellie jumped out of bed. "I'd forgotten!" she squeaked. "Let's go! Can we bring Rascal?" She always loved getting the Christmas tree. Dad had already got the box of decorations out of the loft, she noticed happily, as she dashed downstairs a few minutes later. Mum and Lila and Max were still having a lie-in, but she didn't want to miss this.

"Have some toast!" Dad handed her a jammy slice. "You can take it with you."

They headed out of the house and down the road to the little greengrocer's shop on the high street.

My Naughty Little Puppy

"Can we have a really, really big tree?"
she asked Dad hopefully.

Rascal sniffed a lovely bushy fir tree,
and edged up close, with a look in his eye
that Ellie recognized. "Rascal, no!" she
hissed, and he looked up at her in surprise.
It was a tree – what was the problem?

Dad laughed. "You wee on it, Rascal,
we have to buy it," he told him solemnly.
"How about that one in the corner, Ellie?"

Ellie nodded. It was huge!

My Naughty Little Puppy

They carried the tree back home – or rather Dad carried most of it, and Ellie held the pointy end.

"Now we just need to get it in the stand," Dad said, as they went up the path.

Mum opened the front door, looking horrified. "It's enormous!"

"Isn't it?" said Dad proudly, and Ellie beamed. Rascal barked approvingly.

"It's taller than our living-room ceiling!" Mum exclaimed.

Dad and Ellie looked at the tree doubtfully. "Is it?" Dad asked. "Oh well... Perhaps we can cut a bit off the bottom..."

In the end, the tree *just* fitted, although the fairy on the top had to be at a funny angle. Dad and Ellie spent the whole

morning wrapping it in tinsel, and hanging
on baubles, while Lila pointed out gaps in
the tinsel.

"It's lovely," Ellie said happily, as they
stood back to admire it.

My Naughty Little Puppy

"It looks wonderful," said Mum. "Even if it does take up half the room."

Rascal eyed it suspiciously. He liked trees, but he had a feeling he wasn't allowed to wee on this one either. And Ellie had told him off when he nosed one of the baubles. Why did they swing about so interestingly if he wasn't allowed to play with them?

Chapter Seven

Fun at the Fair

"Are you all ready?" Jo smiled at the little group of dogs and owners standing in the entrance to the village hall, and Ellie glanced round proudly. Everyone had made such an effort!

Jack's mum had sewn Hugo a beautiful red coat with a gold braid trim, which looked amazing against his smooth golden-brown fur. Christy had brought Bouncer in his antlers, which had jingly bells on them.

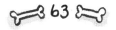

My Naughty Little Puppy

Bouncer was sitting perfectly next to her, with a special collecting tin gripped in his teeth.

Ellie had made it out of a seaside bucket. She'd covered it with red paper, and got Rascal to make paint pawprints on it. She'd hoped Rascal might carry it, but it was a bit big for him, and he'd probably have chewed through the handle anyway.

Rascal was sitting next to Bouncer, eyeing it enviously, with his hat hanging down over one eye as usual. It was looking a bit raggedy now, as he had taken to dragging the hat around with him. Even Amelia had put Goldie in a sparkly red coat.

"Let's start with 'Away in a Manger', since we all know it really well." Ellie looked

at the door nervously. She could see
through the glass panels that people
were lining up outside. They began to
sing as Jo went to open the hall doors.
People started trickling in, stopping to
admire the dogs and drop some change
into Bouncer's bucket.

"What next?" Ellie asked, as they
finished, and Amelia leaped in.

"I want to do my solo for 'Once in
Royal David's City'," she demanded.

Ellie sighed. "OK..."

Amelia closed her eyes, and her face
took on a saintly expression. She began to
sing, and a couple of people stopped to
listen, smiling admiringly. She had just got
to the difficult high bit, when someone else

joined in, and her eyes snapped open
in horror.

"Ahhhrrrooo!" Hugo howled, in a
deep bass voice.

"Hugo, ssshh!" Jack hissed, trying not to
laugh. But Hugo went on howling, and then
Rascal started up too, in a much squeakier
little howl. "Owwwooooo!"

Amelia was bright scarlet – the colour
of her hat – but she carried on singing
grimly to the end of the verse. Then
everyone else joined in, as well as they
could, giggling every so often.

Funnily enough, Hugo and Rascal
stopped as soon as everyone was singing.
"It's only Amelia's voice they don't like!"
Christy whispered to Ellie.

My Naughty Little Puppy

Quite a few people had gathered to listen, and they clapped at the end of the carol.

"Your Great Dane's a star!" one lady told Jack. Lots of people put money in the tin, and patted Rascal and Hugo, and told them how good the dogs' "singing" was.

"You did that on purpose!" Amelia hissed at Jack and Ellie, as their audience went on into the hall.

Jack stared at her. "You think I've trained Hugo to howl when you sing?" he asked.

Amelia was about to argue back when a man with a large camera hanging round his neck came in. "I'm from the local paper," he explained. "Are you carol singing? Can I take a couple of pictures?"

My Naughty Little Puppy

Amelia immediately snapped
a smile back on her face,
and patted Goldie's
ears into the best
position.

"Let's sing 'Jingle
Bells'," Ellie
suggested, knowing
that everyone smiled
in that one.

The man took lots of photos, and then
went on into the hall. Ellie and the others
had just sung all the way through their list of
carols twice when Jo came out to see them,
with a lady in a rescue centre fleece. "You
were fab!" she told them. "This is Carol, she
runs Paws for Thought."

"I just wanted to say thank you!" Carol said, as she patted all the dogs. "The carol singing was such a good idea."

"Why don't you all come and look round the stalls," Jo suggested. "You haven't had a chance to see the rest of the fair, and I think most people are here now."

Ellie nodded. "I'm just going to find Mum and Dad," she told Christy and Lucy. Her family had arrived a few minutes before, and she wanted to go round with them. She was hoping to get something for Max to replace the fudge.

My Naughty Little Puppy

"Hello, Ellie! You sounded lovely," Mum told her. "Aren't these stalls wonderful?"

Ellie nodded, admiring the hats laid out in front of them. They had really cool designs, and she could see Lila fingering one with knitted flowers sewn on to it. She'd already got Lila some nail polish though... Then Ellie spotted the perfect hat for Max - knitted with ears like a dog's, with big eyes and fierce teeth, too. She was sure he'd love it. She quickly fumbled for her purse, and tucked the hat away in her coat pocket before Max could spot it.

Half an hour later, Ellie had a scarf for Grandad from the same stall, with paw prints knitted on it, and a lot of things for Rascal.

My Naughty Little Puppy

She hadn't meant to buy him anything else, but she just couldn't resist. She gave him his new rubber bone straight away, as a reward for his singing, but she was saving the other things for Christmas. Rascal was looking tired, so she scooped him up and carried him around the stalls as he chewed on his bone happily. Ellie was just walking past the Lucky Dip, wondering if Mum or Dad might buy her a cake from the refreshments stall in the corner, as she'd spent all her money, when Rascal spotted Hugo again, and dropped his bone in excitement.

The bone went straight into the big box of shredded paper, just as a little girl was about to reach in for her prize. She looked up in surprise as the bone went past her,

My Naughty Little Puppy

and then gasped as a small brown-and-white dog hurtled past too.

"Rascal!" Ellie cried. She'd been thinking about cake and not holding him very tightly, so he'd simply leaped out of her arms and straight into the Lucky Dip!

"Now *that* is a good picture!" someone said, and the newspaper photographer snapped Rascal, his bone held triumphantly between his teeth.

Chapter Eight

Snow!

"It says the Christmas Fair raised over five hundred pounds," Ellie said proudly, reading the local midweek newspaper that had just come through the door.

"I can't believe Rascal's on the front page," Mum said, chuckling to herself. It was funny. Rascal was looking right at the camera, bright-eyed and half-covered in shredded paper. The Lucky Dip sign was hanging over his head, and it looked like

My Naughty Little Puppy

he'd just dipped and won his bone. *Or maybe he was the prize*, Ellie thought lovingly, stroking the real version, who was lurking by her feet, hoping there might be some food to munch on soon.

"Amelia's going to be so cross," Ellie said smugly. "She was following that photographer around, trying to get him to take pictures of her and Goldie. Actually..." She laughed, and glanced up to show her mum something she'd just noticed at the very back of the photo. "I can see Amelia there in the corner..." Then she squeaked excitedly, and jumped up from the table. "Mum, look!"

"What is it?" Her mum turned round to see. "Oh, goodness..."

"It's snowing, it's snowing! Look at it, it's falling so fast!"

There was a thundering on the stairs, and Max hurtled into the kitchen. "Have you seen? It's snowing! Where's the sledge? Where's my snowboots? Come on, Ellie!" He raced out again, leaving Ellie and Mum open-mouthed, and Rascal staring after him doubtfully.

"He can't possibly go sledging in half a centimetre of snow..." Mum muttered, as Dad came in and peered out of the window.

"It's falling very fast," he said. "I don't think it'll be long before there's plenty of snow for sledging..."

My Naughty Little Puppy

"Rascal's never seen snow before." Ellie picked up Rascal to show him the view out of the kitchen window. Rascal whined, looking at the strange white stuff all over the garden.

My Naughty Little Puppy

Dad was right. It only took about half an hour for there to be a thick layer of snow covering the pavement in front of the house. Max had been standing on the doorstep, clutching the sledge while he watched it settle, and now he popped his head back in to yell for Ellie. "Are you coming to the park, Ellie? Do you want to bring Rascal?"

Ellie flung on her coat and boots, and looked thoughtfully at Rascal, who was jumping around in the hope of a walk. Would he like the snow? It was probably almost up to his tummy by now, in the deep bits. She wrinkled her nose. He was going to have to like it. Who knew how long the snow would last? They couldn't possibly keep him inside the whole time. Rascal got

My Naughty Little Puppy

even rascallier than usual if he didn't have
two good walks a day.

She clipped on his lead and opened the
front door. Rascal went to race out as usual,
but then stopped dead and looked up at
Ellie in confusion.

My Naughty Little Puppy

Ellie put her hand over her mouth to stop herself from laughing at him. Rascal looked completely shocked. But then, everything had changed since they'd popped out for an early-morning walk before breakfast, she realized.

"It's OK, Rascal," she whispered. "It's only snow. It's fun, look." She picked up a handful, and flung it across the garden.

"Does he like it?" Max called.

"I don't think he's sure yet," Ellie told him. "Come on, Rascal." She stepped out on to the path, and led him over to the gate where Max was waiting.

With tiny, dainty steps, Rascal tiptoed into the snow. Ellie had been right. It was almost up to the top of his little legs already.

My Naughty Little Puppy

Max watched Rascal padding along,
and sighed. "This is going to take hours.
Look, you sit on the sledge with him, and I'll
pull you there. That'll give him some time to
get used to it."

"Cool!" Ellie sat down on the sledge,
and hugged Rascal tight. He was as good
as a hot-water bottle in this cold. Rascal
squeaked excitedly as Max set off, and the
sledge ran smoothly along, bouncing here
and there over dips in the snow.

My Naughty Little Puppy

By the time they got to the park, Rascal was less confused by the cold white stuff. He chased after the sledge as Max and Ellie went down the big slope, barking excitedly and half-swimming through the snow as he hit the deep bits.

"OK. I'm exhausted," Max said, a while later. "We must have gone down a hundred times. *And* back up again."

Ellie nodded. "Let's go home and ask Mum for some hot chocolate. I'm frozen. And then we could make a snowman in the garden, maybe. We don't know how long the snow's going to last."

Max nodded, and they set off home, Rascal jumping and wading through the snow beside them.

My Naughty Little Puppy

Mum had been making mince pies, so after a couple of those each, and hot chocolate, they felt recovered enough to go out again.

Lila had been asleep until now, but she got up and came outside just as Max and Ellie were about to start on their snowman.

"Snowmen are boring," she said firmly, in a very big-sister way. "Let's make an igloo."

Ellie looked at the snow doubtfully. There was lots of it, but it was very squishy. She wasn't sure it was good building snow. But Lila was determined, and she soon had Max and Ellie working on a production line, squashing the snow into hard, glittery blocks, so she could arrange them into the shape of an igloo.

My Naughty Little Puppy

"Um, Lila..." Ellie said, after the first few rows. "It's a very small igloo..."

Lila stood back and looked at it. Then she giggled. "It's going to have to be a dogloo..."

"Uurgh, don't tell Rascal that!" Max snorted with laughter.

"You know what I meant!" Lila flung a snowball at him. "Stop being stupid, let's

get it finished. We just need to get the roof filled in."

Rascal pottered out of the house – he'd been recovering from the trip to the park with a snooze on his cushion – and admired the igloo, sniffing all round it. Ellie thought he was about to lift his leg against it, and glared at him, but luckily he decided not to. Lila might have thrown a wobbly if he had.

My Naughty Little Puppy

"Last block!" Lila carefully wedged the final block of snow in place.

Rascal wandered round from the back of the igloo and peered into the little doorway. He looked up at Ellie, as though he wasn't sure he was allowed in.

"Go on, Rascal!" she told him, and he poked his nose in thoughtfully and then went all the way inside, turning round and lying down as though he approved.

Lila took a photo of him on her phone, laughing.

"I'm going to make a snow-dog now," Ellie said, wandering further down the garden to find some fresh snow.

But snow-dogs were difficult, it turned out. The paws kept falling off. And it was getting colder and colder. Lila and Max had already gone inside, and finally she decided it must be close to lunchtime. She looked round for Rascal, but he must have gone in with Lila and Max.

"Oh, I was just going to call you, Ellie!" Mum told her, as she opened the door. Then she frowned. "Where's Rascal?"

"He came in with the others..." Ellie said.

Mum shook her head. "No, he's definitely not here."

Ellie looked back out across the garden worriedly. Had Rascal got out somehow? What if the snow had drifted, and he was stuck, buried in the snow?

Then she smiled. "Wait a minute," she told Mum, and ran to check the dogloo.

My Naughty Little Puppy

Sure enough, there he was. His white bits were blending into the snow, so only his little brown ears stood out in the dim, snowy light inside. Rascal was fast asleep in his own little snow-house.

Chapter Nine

Mince Pies for Rascal

Ellie wrapped up most of her presents on Christmas Eve. She'd given Christy and Lucy their presents the day before, when they went over to Christy's house. Luckily, Christy lived close enough to walk – Mum didn't like driving in the snow. They'd made an enormous snowman in Christy's front garden.

Ellie looked happily at the little pile of presents on her bedroom floor. She had made the wrapping paper herself, and used

My Naughty Little Puppy

glittery Christmas stickers instead of tape.
She'd printed out some more photos of
Rascal in his hat and used them as gift tags,
with some glitter on the hat, and they looked
gorgeous. She was ready to put them under
the tree, just in time for tomorrow!

"Come on, Rascal!" She picked up the
pile, and went to the door, but a worried yip
behind her made her stop. Rascal was trying
to follow her, but he'd been playing with the
roll of ribbon, batting it around with his paws,
rolling over with it, chasing it under the bed...

Then he'd sat down for a little
rest, and somehow the ribbon
had wrapped
around all four
paws.

My Naughty Little Puppy

Ellie put the presents down on her bed. "Maybe I should put *you* under the Christmas tree!" She giggled. "You look just like a present, Rascal! You just need a bow on your head." She undid him carefully, and rolled the ribbon up again, while Rascal pranced around her, happy to be free. The house was full of good smells, and interesting things kept arriving.

Ellie led him downstairs to put the presents under the tree. There were so many! And lots of them had her name on. She'd felt them, but she couldn't tell what was inside. Proudly, she added hers to the pile, and then wandered into the kitchen to see what Mum was doing.

"Oh, yum, more mince pies."

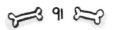

My Naughty Little Puppy

"Well, Max and Lewis between them polished off the rest of the last batch," Mum explained, as she cut out the pastry circles, "and I thought you might want to leave some out for Father Christmas tonight."

My Naughty Little Puppy

Ellie nodded. "And carrots. Have we got any?"

Mum nodded towards the vegetable basket. It was practically overflowing. "The reindeer wouldn't like some sprouts as well, would they? I think your dad got a bit carried away in the supermarket."

"Mum, no one likes sprouts. Not even reindeer. Or Dad! Why did he buy so many?"

"Sprouts are a Christmas thing. We'll all just have a couple..." Mum sighed. "And who knows what we'll do with the other fifty or so..."

There was a strange creaking noise from the living room, followed by a worried whine, and Ellie looked at Mum in horror.

My Naughty Little Puppy

"Rascal! I left him in there alone!"

Ellie raced back into the living room, to find the Christmas tree leaning at a very weird angle. Rascal had tinsel wrapped right the way round his middle, and one of the candy canes that Gran and Grandpa had sent was sticking out of his mouth.

"Oh, Rascal!"

"Is he all right?" Mum asked anxiously, as she hurried into the room. Then she saw Rascal crunching the last of the candy cane and sighed. "Of course he is. What's he done to the tree?"

"Don't worry, Mum. It'll be fine," Ellie said, trying to push the tree straight again. "It's just a bit lopsided..."

"Mum, can we put out the mince pies for Father Christmas now?" Ellie asked. She was just about to go to bed, after staying up late to watch a film with Lila and Max.

"Oh, I already did, Ellie," Mum called apologetically from the sofa. "Sorry, did you want to?"

"Where are they?" Ellie looked at the fireplace, and then noticed that there was an empty plate pushed behind the poinsettia plant Dad had brought home for Mum.

"Not again, Rascal!" Mum said crossly. "Oh, when am I going to stop forgetting about you? I just put them there like we always do. And after the candy cane, as well. If you're sick on Christmas Eve I'm going to take your present back to the shop!" She sighed and got up. "I'll go and get some more. And this time I'm putting them in a tin, with a note! I'm sure Father Christmas won't mind..."

Rascal burped loudly, and then jumped up, looking surprised at himself as though he wasn't sure where the noise had come from.

Ellie giggled and picked him up. She had a feeling it was a good thing it was bedtime!

Chapter Ten

Rascal's Christmas

"Urrgh..." Ellie rolled over, brushing at her damp cheek. "Rascal! What time is it?"

It was still completely dark in her bedroom, and it felt early. "Oh, Rascal! It's only half-past five!" But Rascal was scampering up and down Ellie's bed, whining excitedly. At last, he gave up trying to make Ellie do what he wanted, and seized something in his teeth, dragging it towards her.

My Naughty Little Puppy

"My Christmas stocking! I'd forgotten what day it was!" Ellie was suddenly wide awake. "I'm not sure you're going to want any of it though, Rascal," she told the excited little dog, as she turned on her bedside light. "It'll be pencils and books, and maybe some chocolate..."

She tipped out a little pile of parcels, and Rascal swiftly seized the one he'd been sniffing out. Ellie laughed. "Dog chocolates! OK, I take it back. Shall I open them then?" She held them above his nose, teasingly. "OK, OK! Don't bark, Mum'll make us go back to sleep." She opened the packet, and fed Rascal a few of the dog choc drops, while she ate a chocolate snowman and opened the rest of her stocking presents.

Then she snuggled down to look at one of the books, and the next thing she knew, someone was tickling her.

"I thought you'd slept late for Christmas morning!"

Ellie jumped awake, and looked up to see Dad laughing at her. "What time did you open those, then?"

"Half-five." Ellie yawned. "Rascal woke me up – there was a packet of doggie chocs in my stocking."

"I see! Get dressed now, Ellie. It's breakfast time, and Auntie Gemma, Liam and Grandad will be here soon."

Ellie wriggled out of bed, trying not to tip her presents all over the floor, and dressed quickly. She was hungry, and before she reached the kitchen she could already smell the croissants that Mum had bought for a special Christmas breakfast.

"When can we open our presents?" Max asked.

"Not till everyone else is here," Mum said firmly.

Max sighed and stuffed half a croissant in his mouth in one go. Lila groaned, but Mum pretended she hadn't seen him.

My Naughty Little Puppy

Rascal suddenly bolted down the bit of croissant Ellie had "dropped" for him – it was Christmas – and raced out into the hall.

"I guess people are arriving!" Mum laughed. "He must have heard them coming up the path."

Grandad was at the door, and Auntie Gemma and her boyfriend Liam were just pulling up in their car.

"Happy Christmas, Grandad!" Ellie hugged him. "Come on, I want you to open my present!"

Everyone gathered in the living room. Dad started to hand out presents, and soon the room was full of bits of wrapping paper and ribbon.

"It's beautiful! Can I put it on now?"

Ellie asked, stroking the velvety fabric of her new dress from Mum and Dad.

"Let's open the rest of the presents first," Mum said. "There's a pile here for Rascal. Oh, and this one is for you, Gemma, from all of us."

"Oooh, that looks interesting." Auntie Gemma took the squashy parcel, and started to undo it, while Ellie got Rascal to tear at the wrapping paper on one from his little pile.

"Did you make this, Mum? It's gorgeous!" Rascal sniffed at his first present curiously as Ellie opened it out.

"Well, I thought Hugo looked so nice in his red coat at the fair, Ellie. And it's so cold at the moment, I thought maybe Rascal could do with one."

My Naughty Little Puppy

Ellie wrapped the little blue coat round
Rascal, and did up the Velcro. "It's really
smart. Thanks, Mum!"

"And this is beautiful!" Auntie Gemma
had opened her present now, a lovely
knitted red hat. "I need a hat."

"To keep your other hats company?"
Liam teased her. "It is nice, though.

My Naughty Little Puppy

And thanks for the books, they look great."

Grandad wrapped his new scarf round his neck, and kissed Ellie. "Lovely. Very cosy, Ellie, I love it. And look at Max's hat, that's very smart."

"It's cool, Ellie, great teeth!" Max pulled it on. "That'll be good for when we go sledging again."

My Naughty Little Puppy

"Have we really opened all that huge pile?" Mum shook her head in amazement. "Wow. Actually, I need to go and check on the turkey."

Rascal trotted after her. The smells from the kitchen were so good, he didn't want to miss anything.

Ellie went and changed into her dress, then spent the rest of the morning nibbling chocolate snowmen, and playing Max's new PlayStation game with him. He beat her every time, which meant he was happy. Lila watched them, and painted one fingernail in each of the ten colours in the set Ellie had given her, to see which she liked best.

"Lunch!" Mum called eventually, and everyone squashed into the kitchen.

My Naughty Little Puppy

"Yay, crackers!" Max grabbed his, and

waved it at
Ellie. It went
off with a
huge bang
when they
pulled it, and
Rascal yelped and
scooted out of the kitchen.

"Oh dear..." Ellie got up to follow him,
but Mum called her back. "He's better off
out there, Ellie. There are more crackers,
and I don't want him begging at the table."

They were just having a little rest
between the turkey and the Christmas
pudding, when Auntie Gemma gave a cry
of horror. "Oh no! My beautiful hat!"

My Naughty Little Puppy

"What is it? What's the matter?" Mum asked worriedly, looking where Auntie Gemma was looking.

"Oh, I just don't believe it..."

Rascal had come back into the kitchen. He was sitting on his cushion, staring back at Auntie Gemma in surprise as she pointed at him, with a shredded-looking red hat dangling out of his mouth.

Ellie put her hand over her mouth, horrified, but then she looked closer and burst out laughing. She stopped as Mum glared at her. "It's OK! It isn't your hat, Auntie Gemma. Honestly! It's the Santa hat I made Rascal."

"The one in that lovely photo you gave me?" Grandad asked.

My Naughty Little Puppy

"Yes, it's his favourite thing. I gave him loads of new toys for Christmas, but he still wants to eat his tatty old hat!"

Auntie Gemma sighed with relief. "I'm sorry, Rascal, sweetheart. When I saw the red material... And you have to admit he's got a history, Ellie. My handbag's never been the same since Rascal got his paws on it!""

"Let's have the Christmas pudding," Mum said hastily, bringing it over to the table. "Mind you don't eat the charms, everybody."

She served it out carefully.

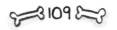

"Oh!" Auntie Gemma went pink, as she held up the silver ring, and Liam gave her a hug, and whispered something in her ear. Everyone else stared at them hopefully, but they didn't say anything more.

Ellie beamed – maybe she might be a bridesmaid soon! She spooned through her serving, wondering if any of the little silver figures were in it. "I've got one!" she squeaked excitedly, spotting a strand of red ribbon. "Oh, it's the dog!"

Lila grinned. "So Ellie has to clear up after Rascal for the whole year!"

Ellie didn't mind. She scooped Rascal up and hugged him. The dog charm was just what she'd wanted – it meant a wonderful new year full of adventures with Rascal!